LITTLE JEEMES HENRY

By Ellis Credle

DOWN DOWN THE MOUNTAIN

ACROSS THE COTTON PATCH

LITTLE JEEMES HENRY

PRINTED IN THE UNITED STATES OF AMERICA
BY THE POLYGRAPHIC COMPANY OF AMERICA, N.Y.

LITTLE JEEMES HENRY

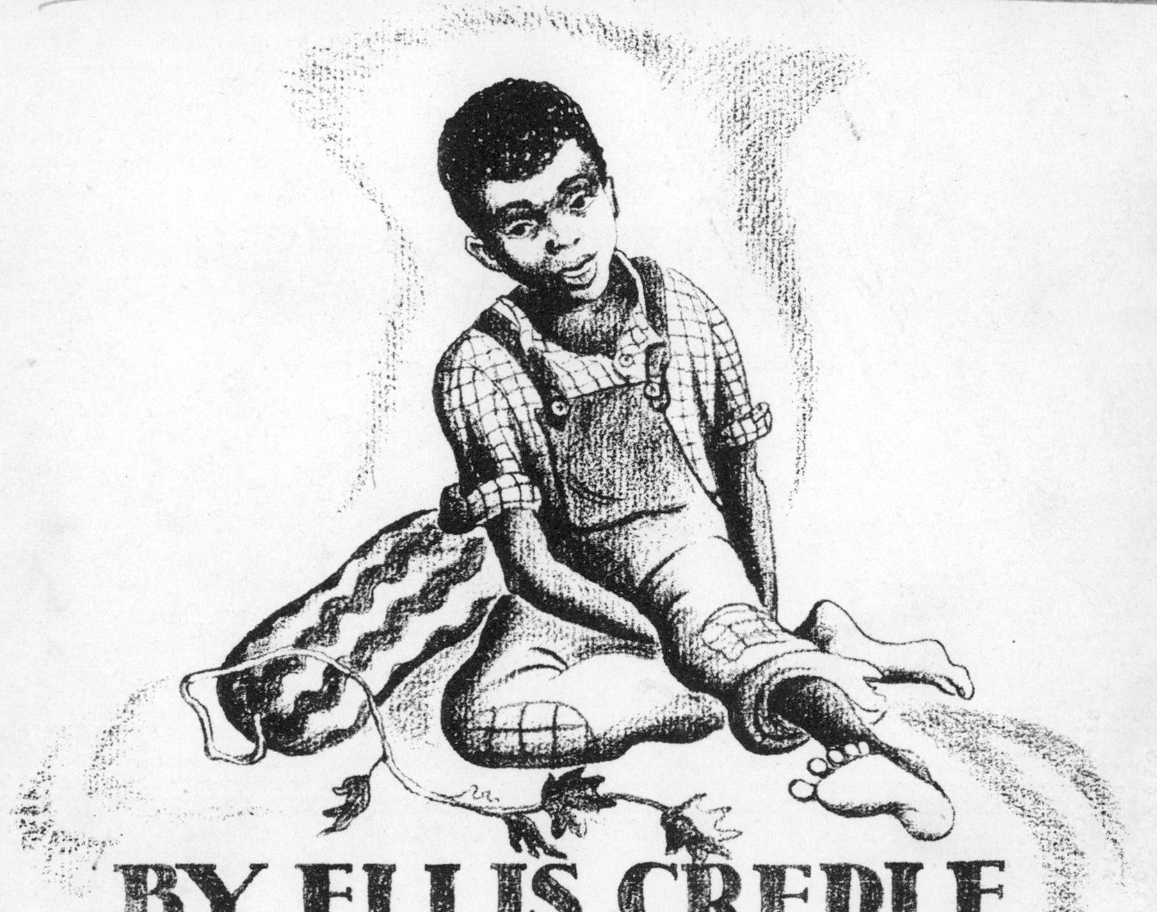

BY ELLIS CREDLE

This special edition is published by
E. M. HALE AND COMPANY
by special arrangement with the
publisher of the regular edition, THOMAS NELSON and SONS
New York

LITTLE JEEMES HENRY

Little Jeemes Henry lived with his Pappy and his Mammy in a little house in the middle of a white cotton patch. Jeemes Henry played all day long while his Pappy worked in the field and his Mammy kept house.

Then one day his Pappy came in from the field. "Mammy," said he, "Ah cain't make no cash money on dis farm. Ah wants to go off and git myself a job and make a pocketful of money. Reckon you can carry on de farm by yo'self for a while?"

"Reckon Ah kin," said Mammy. "Jeemes Henry, he's a smart boy, he kin help me."

And so Pappy packed his suitcase and away he went to get a job and make a pocketful of money for Mammy and little Jeemes Henry.

After that, little Jeemes Henry had to help with everything. He had to work in the tobacco and the corn and the cotton and there never seemed to be any time to play. And it was very dull without his Pappy around the place.

But one day as Mammy and Jeemes Henry were picking cotton, a strange man came along the road. Past the cotton patch he trudged and up the hill to the tobacco barns. He got out some big rolls of bright colored paper and began pasting them on the side of the barn.

"Look at dat white man," said little Jeemes Henry. "Look lak he pastin' a great big enormous picture on dat barn!"

"It's de picture of de circus dat's comin' to de town," explained Mammy.

"Gee whiz, Mammy!" cried little Jeemes Henry, "Ah sho' do wish Ah could go to dat circus! Look at all dem animals and dat lady standin' up on dat hoss's back! Look at dem monkeys and ever'thing!"

"Wish you could go, son," said Mammy, "but it take fifty cents to git a ticket to dat circus, and dat's a heap o' money if you ain't got it!"

"Maybe my Pappy come back wid a pocketful o' money. He take me to dat circus," said little Jeemes Henry.

"Don't 'speck he'll git back in time," said Mammy. "It take a long time to git a job and make a pocketful o' money."

"Maybe Ah kin think up some way to make dat fifty cents my own self," said little Jeemes Henry.

"Maybe you kin, son," agreed Mammy. "You go ahaid and think hard."

And little Jeemes Henry thought. He thought and thought and thought. "Mammy," he said at last, "dat old guinea hen o' yourn done hid her nest so dat you cain't never find it, ain't she?"

"Son, she sho' have!"

"Well Mammy, if Ah finds dat nest, kin Ah have all de eggs to sell in de store?" asked little Jeemes Henry.

"Dat you kin, son, but Ah don't speck you kin find dat nest."

"Ah look," said Jeemes Henry.

At sunset, Jeemes Henry and his Mammy set out for home. Mammy went into the little cabin to cook supper and Jeemes Henry began to search everywhere for the guinea hen's nest.

He poked among the bushes and scratched among the honeysuckle vines. He searched and he searched. But when his Mammy called him home to supper, he had not seen a sign of the guinea hen's nest.

Little Jeemes Henry was a bit down-hearted. He hardly felt like eating his cornbread and molasses.

"You ain't seen no sign o' dat nest, is you?" asked Mammy.

"No'm, Ah ain't, but Ah gwine keep on lookin'!"

E·A·C

But just then, in a clump of dog fennel, he spied a neat round nest.

"Whoopee!" yelled little Jeemes Henry. He gathered the eggs into his hat and away he went home.

He burst into the cabin where Mammy was cooking breakfast. "Laws-a-mussy!" cried Mammy, "if dat boy ain't found de guinea hen's nest!"

"Is dis 'nuff eggs to buy a ticket to de circus?" cried little Jeemes Henry.

"Sho' 'tis!" said Mammy. "When us git outen de field at twelve o'clock, you kin take dem eggs to de store and git de money!"

So that day at noontime, Jeemes Henry put the eggs carefully into a basket and started for the store. The burning sun shone down and the dirt on the road was blistering hot. Little Jeemes Henry hopped from one bare foot to another.

"Ah'll haf to run," thought he. "If Ah don't git outen dis hot dirt my foots gwine be baked lak a 'tatter!" So he held tight to his basket of eggs and went running as fast as he could go. But still the dirt kept burning his feet.

"Got to git outen here!" cried he, and away he went faster and faster. Suddenly Jeemes Henry tripped over his own big feet!

Down he went in a big cloud of dust!

"Oh my guinea eggs!" thought poor little Jeemes Henry, and he closed his eyes tight because he was afraid to look. But at last he opened them. There were the eggs, broken and streaming all over Jeemes Henry from head to foot.

Big tears came into Jeemes Henry's eyes and made streaks on his dusty black face. He felt almost too miserable to go home. But after a while he got up and started. He crept in the field where Mammy was picking cotton.

"What under de sun done happen to you, chile?" she cried when she saw Jeemes Henry.

"Done fell down and busted all dem eggs," stammered poor little Jeemes Henry.

"Laws-a-mussy!" cried Mammy. "Now how you gwine git yo' circus ticket, Jeemes Henry?"

"Dunno, Mammy," said little Jeemes Henry.

All that afternoon he tried not to look at the picture on the barn, but the monkeys seemed to wink and the lady on the horse seemed to smile at him.

Perhaps he could think of another way to earn that fifty cents. That night he went to bed early. He lay awake and thought and thought. Outside in the dark, all the little bugs were singing, "Cir-cus, cir-cus, cir-cus!" and all the little beetles were fiddling, "Cir-cus, cir-cus, cir-cus!" They played the same tune over and over until at last little Jeemes Henry fell asleep.

ELLIS CREDLE

The next morning he was up bright and early. He sat down to breakfast and helped himself to a plate full of hot batter-cakes. He plastered them with butter and covered them with molasses.

"Mammy," he said between big bites, "Ah done thought how to make another fifty cents!"

"How dat?" asked Mammy.

"Ah gwine watch de gate to de white folks' house and when dey comes drivin' out in de autymobile, Ah gwine run open de gate for 'em! Dey allus gives me a penny when Ah does dat, and sometimes dey gives me a nickel. Ah save all dem pennies and nickels and fo' long Ah have fifty cents!"

"Dat's de truf!" cried Mammy. "You sho' is one bright boy!"

And so that day, as Jeemes Henry picked cotton, he kept an eye on the big house where the white folks lived. It was not long before he saw Mr. Moore back his car out of the garage and come driving toward the gate.

Jeemes Henry dropped his bag of cotton. He dashed across the road and swung the gate wide open.

"Thank you, Jeemes Henry," said Mr. Moore, and he fished into his pocket and found a bright new penny for little Jeemes Henry.

Jeemes Henry bowed and scraped and showed all his white teeth. Then he ran back to the cotton patch and showed the penny to his Mammy.

"All Ah got to have now is foty-nine mo'!" cried Jeemes Henry joyfully.

"You just keep at it," urged Mammy. "You'll git 'em!"

And Jeemes Henry kept at it. Every day his little pile of coins grew higher and higher. At last there were enough to buy a ticket to the circus. How happy Jeemes Henry felt then!

"Now Ah got de money, who gwine take me to de circus?" asked little Jeemes Henry.

"Don't you worry 'bout dat," said Mammy. "Dey be plenty folks gwine to dat circus. When us goes to preachin' on Sunday, Ah ax somebody to take you 'long."

When Sunday came, Mammy and Jeemes Henry dressed up in their Sunday clothes. Jeemes Henry took his circus money and tied it into a beautiful red handkerchief. Then he placed it proudly in the pocket of his pink blouse.

They started for the church. How grand Jeemes Henry felt as he went singing along with a whole half dollar in his pocket!

GOD MADE DE BEAUTIFUL SUNSHINE—
DE MOON TO ROLL ON HIGH
DE VERY LAST THING
DAT HE DID MAKE
WAS THE WINDSTORM
IN THE SKY
LITTLE DAVID
PLAY ON YO' HARP
PLAY ON YO' HARP
OF GOLD

It was not very long before they came to the church. All the colored folks from miles around were there. The first one they met was Cousin Garfield.

"Howdy, Cousin Garfield," Mammy greeted him. "Is you gwine to de circus next Tuesday?"

"Sho' is," replied Cousin Garfield. "Gwine hitch up de mule to de wagon and take my whole fambly!"

"Sho' nuff!" said Mammy. "Does you speck you got nuff room to take little Jeemes Henry 'long?"

"Sho has,' said Cousin Garfield. "Ah stop by yo' house bright and early Tuesday mornin'. Ah take little Jeemes Henry and put him right in 'mongst my own chilluns!"

Little Jeemes Henry grinned from ear to ear, and he felt of the money in his pocket to make sure that it was still safely there.

ELLIS-CREDLE

Then it was time for preaching to begin. The colored folk trooped into the little church. Jeemes Henry sat right on the front row where he could see everything.

How grand it was in the church! On one wall was a big banner. "Welcome Sinners" it said in bright gold letters. But the most beautiful thing of all was the window behind the pulpit. The sun shone through its colored panes, making them shine like rubies and diamonds and emeralds.

The minister called out the name of a song and everybody sang. And how they sang! The little church almost rocked with the sound.

Little Jeemes Henry began to feel very happy and he opened his mouth and sang as loud as anybody.

Then the minister began his sermon. "We gwine drive Ole Man Sin away from here!" he shouted.

And all the colored folk answered, "Yas Lawd!"

"Whippin' de Old Man round de stump!" cried the preacher.

"Yas Lawd!" shouted all the people and little Jeemes Henry shouted with them.

"Got 'im on de run!" cried the preacher.

"Yas Lawd!" yelled all the people.

Little Jeemes Henry yelled too. And he began to feel very warm. His shoes felt so tight that he took them off and held them in his lap.

"Dare go Ole Man Sin!" shouted the preacher. "Done drove him clean away!"

ELLIS CREDLE

"Yas Lawdy! Whoopee!" The colored folk shouted and clapped their hands. They stood up and threw their hats into the air. Little Jeemes Henry stood up and threw his shoes into the air.

Then there was a terrible crash. One of Jeemes Henry's shoes had gone through a beautiful red windowpane.

All the colored folk stopped shouting. They stared at the hole in their beautiful window. The preacher turned around and looked too.

"Breddern and Sistern," he said, "somebody done busted our wonderful colored window. Now folkses dat windowpane costed fifty cents. If de one what busted dat pane is got dat much money, Ah gwine ax him to come up atter preachin' and pay fo' dat pane. Didn't see who done it folks, but de Good Lawd, he seed you and he gazin' right at you!"

Little Jeemes Henry hung his head. But after preaching he walked up to the pulpit. "Dat wuz my shoe what broke de window," said he. "Here my fifty-cent piece."

On the way home, Jeemes Henry did not say a word. He looked down at the dusty road.

"Don't you be so down-hearted honey," comforted Mammy. "When us git home, Ah gwine cook you some nice cornpone and collards fo' yo' supper."

But little Jeemes Henry could not eat any supper.

"Got to think o' some way to make another fifty cents," he said, and he put his head into his hands and thought and thought.

"Wish Ah could find yo' Pappy," sighed Mammy. "He'd git de money to take you to dat circus!"

"But Pappy he ain't here. Got to git de money my own self," said little Jeemes Henry. "Circus come day atter tomorrow. Ain't got but one mo' day!" The more Jeemes Henry thought, the sleepier he got, and after a while he went to bed.

And while he was asleep, Jeemes Henry had a dream. He thought he went into the woods and there were all the blackberry bushes hanging with bright fifty-cent pieces!

Then he woke up. It was bright sunlight. Little Jeemes Henry jumped up and hustled into his clothes. When he sat down to breakfast his Mammy noticed that his teeth were showing in a broad white grin.

"You looks mighty cheerful, dis mawnin', Jeemes Henry," said she.

"Ah's got a idee!" said little Jeemes Henry proudly.

"What dat?" asked Mammy.

ELLIS CREDLE

"Gwine out in de woods and pick some blackberries. Bet Ah kin sell dem berries to de white folks fo' fifty cents!"

"Yas suh! Bet you kin!" cried Mammy. She gave Jeemes Henry two big buckets and away he went.

In the woods he found the bushes bending with ripe blackberries. But it took him a long time to fill his buckets. The sun was mighty hot and pretty soon the mosquitoes found little Jeemes Henry. They sang around his ears. They bit his arms and his legs and his neck. But Jeemes Henry kept right on picking. The briars scratched him and the perspiration rolled off in big drops, but little Jeemes Henry did not stop. He picked and he picked all day long until both buckets were full. Then he staggered out of the woods and along the road to the white folks' house. Up the path he went with his two big buckets, and he knocked at the back door.

Miss Mary Moore's cook stuck her head out. "What you want, Jeemes Henry?" she asked.

"Ah wants to know does de white folks want to buy any blackberries?" said Jeemes Henry.

"Naw dey don't!" cried the cook. "You go 'way fum here wid dem buckets. First thing you know dese white folks'll have me standin' over de hot stove cookin' blackberry jam!"

Little Jeemes Henry shifted from one foot to the other. "Whar Miss Mary?" he asked.

"Never mind whar she is!" shouted the cook. "Git!" and she hustled out the door and shooed little Jeemes Henry away.

Jeemes Henry shuffled sadly around the house and sat on the front lawn. If he could only see Miss Mary she would certainly buy his berries. He sat for a long time, scratching his head and wondering if he dare go up and knock on the front door. Then suddenly Miss Mary came out on the porch.

"Why heigh-oh, Jeemes Henry," said she. "What have you got in those big buckets?"

Jeemes Henry jumped up. "Ah got some nice blackberries, Miss Mary." He lugged his buckets to the edge of the porch. "Thought maybe you mought want some blackberry jam," said he.

"Why indeed I do!" said Miss Mary. "How much do you want for your blackberries?"

"Ah take fifty cents," said Jeemes Henry fearfully.

Miss Mary went into the house and returned with a bright fifty-cent piece. She gave it to little Jeemes Henry.

"Cook! Cook!" she called. "Come get little Jeemes Henry's buckets, we're going to have some nice blackberry jam for supper!"

Jeemes Henry did not wait. He dashed away as fast as he could go. When he got home he showed the money to his Mammy.

"You is one evermore smart boy!" cried she. "You gwine to dat circus sho' as you bawn! Come on now it gittin' dark. You got to wash yo' foots and git in bed. Tomorrow circus day and you is got to git up early."

Little Jeemes Henry was almost too excited to sleep, but after a while he closed his eyes. When he opened them again, the sun was shining brightly. This was circus day!

Little Jeemes Henry jumped out of bed in a hurry. No sooner was he dressed than he heard the jingle of the chains on Cousin Garfield's mule.

Cousin Garfield pulled up in front of the house. His wagon was loaded down with happy singing colored folk.

"Whoa!" he cried, hauling on the reins. "Come on, Jeemes Henry! Always room fo' one mo'!"

Little Jeemes Henry climbed up.

He sat on the tail end of the wagon and dangled his feet happily.

On they jogged, singing and laughing.

"Gwine to de circus! Whoopee!" shouted little Jeemes Henry.

After a time they came to the town. The mule's feet went clap-clap-clatter on the pavement. And then in no time they were at the circus ground. Bands were playing, balloons were bobbing everywhere and flags were flying in the breeze. A huge brown tent stood in the middle of the field. And so many people milled around that little Jeemes Henry was in a daze.

All the colored folk began piling out of the wagon. Little Jeemes Henry jumped out too.

The whole jolly bunch began pushing through the great crowd. Little Jeemes Henry tried to follow them, but people pressed in all around him and cut him off from his friends. He tried to fight his way through the crowd, but thousands of legs pushed against him and thousands of feet trampled all around him. Pretty soon little Jeemes Henry lost sight of Cousin Garfield and his friends. He could not see anything but strange people all around him.

ELLIS CREDLE

Poor little Jeemes Henry began to cry. Tears came to his eyes and rolled down his little black cheeks. He was lost in that great big crowd!

Then he caught sight of the flag floating from the top of the big circus tent. Little Jeemes Henry stopped crying. He put his hand into his pocket and closed it tightly around his fifty-cent piece.

"Ah done earned dis money all by myself," said he. "Guess Ah kin git in dat circus tent all by myself too!" And on he went, pushing along with the crowd. After a while he came to the door of the big circus tent.

There stood a man in a tall silk hat. "This way for the big show!" he was shouting. "See all the animals and the three-ringed circus besides! Two big shows all for the price of fifty cents! Step up folks and BUY YOUR TICKETS!"

Little Jeemes Henry stepped up. He held out his fifty-cent piece. "Ah wants one o' dem tickets, Mister!" he said bravely.

"Here you are, sonny," said the man. "Walk right in!"

Little Jeemes Henry walked in.

Never in all his life had Jeemes Henry seen so many strange and wonderful animals. There were zebras and lions and monkeys and giraffes and panthers and elephants and a hundred others. Little Jeemes Henry walked around and looked at them all.

There were all sorts of queer people, too. There was a great giant as tall as the tent pole and a little midget no bigger than a doll. And there was a wild man, a yelling, kicking, wild man. Little Jeemes Henry stopped in front of his cage. The wild man shook his bushy head and roared at the crowd.

Little Jeemes Henry looked and looked. Something about that wild man reminded him of his Pappy.

"But Pappy never let his hair git bushy lak dat," said little Jeemes Henry. "And he sho' never wore no earrings!" Jeemes Henry was puzzled. He took hold of the bars and gazed at the wild man.

The wild man caught sight of little Jeemes Henry. He stopped his roaring and stared.

"Why little Jeemes Henry, honey," said the wild man, "what you doin' here all by yo' little self?"

"Done got lost fum Cousin Garfield," explained little Jeemes Henry.

"Well you better come here and git into dis cage wid me," said the wild man. "Pretty soon Ah be through here and Ah take you in de big show and git you de highest seat in de whole tent!"

Little Jeemes Henry thought a little. "Is you de wild man or is you my Pappy?" he asked.

"Ah yo' Pappy," said the man in the cage. "Ah just actin' wild 'cause dat's de job Ah got wid de circus."

He opened the cage door and little Jeemes Henry climbed in. He felt very strange sitting in that cage, but Pappy had promised to find him a high seat in the big show and so little Jeemes Henry waited.

Fewer and fewer people passed through the animal tent, and pretty soon there was nobody at all except little Jeemes Henry and his Pappy. Then Pappy let himself out of the cage.

"Come on Jeemes Henry," said he, "whilst Ah go in my dressin' tent and change my clothes."

Jeemes Henry followed his Pappy. He sat and watched while Pappy took off his earrings and slicked his hair and put on a fine new suit.

Then away they went across the animal tent and in through the door to the big show. There they met Cousin Garfield who was looking everywhere for little Jeemes Henry. How surprised he was to see Jeemes Henry with his Pappy.

"Boy!" cried Cousin Garfield. "Here you is! And if here ain't yo' Pappy what been gone so long!"

"Yas suh! Here Ah is," said Pappy. "Got a job wid de circus. Makin' a pocketful o' money!" Then he led the way to the top row of seats where they could see everything.

Little Jeemes Henry was all eyes. The elephants marched grandly around the ring. Men in red tights turned somersaults in the air right over Jeemes Henry's head. Clowns stumbled and tumbled and the colored folk roared with laughter. Little Jeemes Henry laughed as loud as anybody.

"Boom!" went a huge cannon and out shot a man into the air.

"Whiz!" the monkeys went pedaling around the ring on little bicycles.

"Clippety clop!" the milk-white horses went galloping around with pretty ladies standing up on their backs.

Jeemes Henry's eyes got bigger and bigger. He tried to look everywhere at once. The colored folk clapped and shouted, and little Jeemes Henry clapped and shouted louder than anybody.

Then before he knew it, it was all over. All the colored folk began filing out the front door. But Pappy led little Jeemes Henry through the back tent flap where all the shining circus people were.

"Look, everybody! Dis my little Jeemes Henry!" cried Pappy.

The beautiful circus folk crowded around the little colored boy. A spotted clown hoisted him to his shoulder. A pretty lady gave him a feather from her hair and the tight-rope walker gave him a red balloon. Everybody asked him questions.

But little Jeemes Henry was too happy to say a single word. He just rolled his big eyes and grinned until all his white teeth showed.

Then it was time to go home. Pappy and Jeemes Henry said goodby to all the circus folk, and hustled outside. Cousin Garfield was waiting with his wagon. Pappy and little Jeemes Henry climbed in.

ELLIS CREDLE

"Did you see all dem circus folks close up?" asked all the colored folk eagerly.

"Sho did!" said little Jeemes Henry proudly. "Set right on dat ole clown's shoulder!"

"Uh-uh!" breathed all the colored folk.

"And Pappy he done had a big job in dat circus," bragged Jeemes Henry. "Look what fine clothes he got!"

"Uh-uh! Sho' has!" said all the colored folk and they moved over and gave Pappy and little Jeemes Henry the best seats in the wagon.

In all his life Jeemes Henry had never had such a big day. But now he was tired. He watched the sun sinking down behind the white cotton fields. Then he laid his head on Pappy's shoulder. Jeemes Henry closed his eyes for just a minute.

When he opened them again, he was in his own little cabin, and there was Mammy holding up a lighted lamp.

"Why you little Jeemes Henry!" cried Mammy. "You done brought yo' Pappy home!"

"Sho' has," said little Jeemes Henry sleepily. "And Pappy got a pocketful o' money."

ELLIS CREDLE